Monkey Fun

by Elizabeth Field
illustrated by Dave Blanchette

Printed in the United States of America

ISBN 0-15-317216-9 – Monkey Fun

Ordering Options
ISBN 0-15-318603-8 (Package of 5)
ISBN 0-15-316985-0 (Grade 1 Package)

2 3 4 5 6 7 8 9 10 179 02 01 00

Little monkey in a tree,
Like a bird in flight,
You jump across the trees all day.
What do you do at night?

1

Little monkey in a tree,
Tell me what you hear.

Is it a bird or snake or cat?
Or just your mom who's near?

3

Little monkey in a tree,
Swinging by your tail,

You swing from branch to branch.
Through the trees you sail!

Little monkey in a tree,
Did you disappear?

Or are you playing hide-and-seek
In the tree tops here?

Little monkey in a tree,
Jump down to the ground!

Or do you like to stay up high?
What is that you've found?

9

Little monkey in a tree,
You found fruit to eat.

You pop the fruit into your mouth.
Is it nice and sweet?

11

Little monkey in a tree,
You shook your head at me.
Look ahead and all around.
Tell me what you see!

Teacher/Family Member ·····································

Monkey See, Monkey Do!
Remind your child that monkeys like to imitate the actions of others.
Then play a game together. Take turns pantomiming actions for each
other to mimic.

 School-Home Connection
Ask your child to read *Monkey Fun* to you. Help your child create new
pages for the book.

Word Count:	154
Vocabulary Words:	disappear
	across
	ground
	mouth
	shook
Phonic Elements:	Short Vowel: /e/*ea*
	head
	ahead
	Long Vowel: /ī/*igh*
	flight
	night
	high

···

TAKE-HOME BOOK
Set Sail
Use with "Baboon."

Take-Home Books

Fly Away!

by Dana Catharine
illustrated by Bill Ogden

THIS BOOK IS THE PROPERTY OF:

STATE _____

PROVINCE _____

COUNTY _____

PARISH _____

SCHOOL DISTRICT _____

OTHER _____

Book No. _____

Enter information
in spaces
to the left as
instructed

ISSUED TO	Year Used	CONDITION	
		ISSUED	RETURNED

**PUPILS to whom this textbook is issued must not write on any page
or mark any part of it in any way, consumable textbooks excepted.**

1. Teachers should see that the pupil's name is clearly written in ink in the spaces above in
   every book issued.
2. The following terms should be used in recording the condition of the book: New; Good;
   Fair; Poor; Bad.